DRAGONFLY BOOKS

This Dragonfly Book belongs to:

Armando

allow children to think . . . to imagine . . . to dream.

SCELIDOSAURUS

(ske-LI-doh-SAW-rus)

TYRANNOSAURUS

(tie-RAN-oh-SAW-rus)

TRICERATOPS

(try-SER-a-tops)

STEGOSAURUS

(STEG-oh-SAW-rus)

PTERODACTYL

(TER-oh-DAC-til)

APATOSAURUS

(a-PAT-oh-SAW-rus)

ANCHISAURUS

(AN-ki-SAW-rus)

In memory of Mason Jones and for all of his friends
at Deri Primary School, Bargoed, who miss him very much —I.W.

For Calum —A.R.

The Library of Congress has cataloged the hardcover edition of this work as follows:
Whybrow, Ian. Harry and the dinosaurs go to school / Ian Whybrow ; illustrated by Adrian Reynolds.
p. cm.
Summary: On Harry's first day at his new school he is not sure whether or not to bring his bucket of dinosaurs,
but in the end the dinosaurs help him make a friend.
ISBN 978-0-375-84180-4 (trade)
[1. First day of school—Fiction. 2. Schools—Fiction. 3. Dinosaurs—Fiction. 4. Toys—Fiction.]
I. Reynolds, Adrian, ill. II. Title.
PZ7.W6225Hans 2007 [E]—dc22
2006025438
ISBN 978-0-553-53400-9 (trade pbk.) — ISBN 978-0-553-53401-6 (ebook)
MANUFACTURED IN CHINA
10 9 8 7 6 5 4 3 2
First Dragonfly Books Edition

Harry and the Dinosaurs Go to School

Ian Whybrow and Adrian Reynolds

Dragonfly Books ——————— New York

It was a big day for Harry. He was starting at his new school.
He was very excited because one of his friends, Charlie, was
starting that day, too.

Stegosaurus said he didn't want to go. Not after Triceratops
told him that there were no "Raahhs" allowed in class.
Mom said not to worry—school would be fine.

Harry blew his whistle. Then, just like a teacher, he said, "In twos, holding hands, my dinosaurs. No talking and jump in the bucket."

All the dinosaurs did what Harry said. All except Stegosaurus. He was so nervous, all his plates were rattling. Harry had to give him a special hug.

Sam said, "You can't take dinosaurs to school, silly!"
That's why her toast fell on the floor.

Mom took Harry to school.

Mrs. Rance was waiting at the classroom door when
Harry and Mom got there.

"Hello, Harry," she said. "Welcome to your new school."

Harry said goodbye to Mom, and Mrs. Rance showed
Harry the coat pegs.

"You can leave your lunchbox here, too," she said.

Harry was too shy to ask if he could bring his bucket,
and that's why his dinosaurs got left outside the classroom.

Harry missed his dinosaurs, so he didn't like the classroom, or the art corner, or his special work tray.

And he felt sorry for another new boy with a digger who cried when his mom went home. The boy wouldn't say one single word. Not even his name.

Harry sort of liked the playground at playtime. But even the monkey bars were not much fun without his dinosaurs.

Back in class, the digger boy still wouldn't speak.
"Maybe he wants to go to the bathroom," Harry
suggested. "Can I show him where it is?"

Mrs. Rance said, "Good idea. That's very nice of
you, Harry."

All the way to the bathroom, the boy kept quiet.
It was the same on the way back, till they got to the
coats. Then they heard a voice, very sad and very soft.
"Raaaaaaaaaaaaaahh!" it said.

"That's my dinosaurs," said Harry. "They miss me. Would you like to meet them?"

The boy nodded.

So Harry said, "This is my Apatosaurus and my Anchisaurus and my Scelidosaurus."

"This is Triceratops and Tyrannosaurus. Pterodactyl is the baby. Wait! Where's Stegosaurus?"

"Jump out, Stegosaurus," called Harry. "Don't be shy!"

But Stegosaurus wanted to whisper something in Harry's ear.

"Ah," said Harry. "Stegosaurus says he will only come out if he can have a ride on your digger."

And do you know what? The boy nodded and passed it over.

When Harry and the boy got back, Mrs. Rance said,
"Oh, good! Dinosaurs! I love dinosaurs. Do they 'Raaahh'?"

"RAAAAAAAAAAAAHH!" said the dinosaurs, and blew all the windows open.
"My goodness!" said Mrs. Rance. "That *was* a 'Raaahh'!"

They all sat down in the classroom.
"Now we are going to make new labels for our coat pegs," said Mrs. Rance. "Who knows how to write their name? Hands up."

The boy with the digger put up his hand.
"And what are you going to write?" said Mrs. Rance
with a smile.
"Jackosaurus!" said the boy.
It was the very first word he had spoken all day.
And what a good joke, too!
All the other children laughed and laughed.

Harry felt very happy.
He and his new friend sat down together at a
table with the dinosaurs and Charlie.

They laughed and they "Raaahhed" and they
made beautiful labels to show where they belonged.

ENDOSAURUS

SCELIDOSAURUS

(ske-LI-doh-SAW-rus)

TYRANNOSAURUS

(tie-RAN-oh-SAW-rus)

TRICERATOPS

(try-SER-a-tops)

STEGOSAURUS

(STEG-oh-SAW-rus)

PTERODACTYL

(TER-oh-DAC-til)

APATOSAURUS

(a-PAT-oh-SAW-rus)

ANCHISAURUS

(AN-ki-SAW-rus)

DRAGONFLY
BOOKS

Dragonfly Books introduce children
to the pleasures of caring about and sharing books.
With Dragonfly Books, children will discover
talented artists and writers and
the worlds they have created,
ranging from first concept books to
read-together stories to books for
newly independent readers.

One of the best gifts a child can receive
is a book to read and enjoy.
Sharing reading with children today
benefits them now and in the future.

Begin building your child's future . . .
one Dragonfly Book at a time.

For help in selecting books your child will love,
look for these themes on the back cover of every
Dragonfly Book:

CLASSICS (Including Caldecott Award Winners)
CONCEPTS (Alphabet, Counting, and More)
CULTURAL DIVERSITY
DEATH AND DYING
FAMILY
FASCINATING PEOPLE
FRIENDSHIP
GROWING UP
JUST FOR FUN
MYTHS AND LEGENDS
NATURE AND OUR ENVIRONMENT
OUR HISTORY (Nonfiction and Historical Fiction)
POETRY
SCHOOL
SPORTS